Beau Beaver Goes To Town

Story By

Frances Bloxam

Illustrated By

Jim Sollers

With thanks to Paula and Jim, who have beaver neighbors
Thanks to Jim S., who told me the tale
And thanks always to Big Dog, who named Beau

Story © 2009 by Frances Bloxam.
Illustrations © 2009 by Jim Sollers. All rights reserved.

Library of Congress Cataloging-in-Publication Data
Bloxam, Frances.
  Beau Beaver goes to town / story by Frances Bloxam ; illustrations by Jim Sollers.
      p. cm.
  Summary: Beau Beaver sets out on his own to build his very first dam,
but unfortunately he chooses a spot that simply will not do. Includes facts about beavers.
  ISBN 978-0-89272-792-6 (hardcover : alk. paper)
  [1. Stories in rhyme. 2. Beavers--Fiction. 3. Dams--Fiction.] I. Sollers, Jim, 1951- ill. II. Title.
  PZ8.3.B59843Be 2008
  [E]--dc22
                            2008038375

Design by Rich Eastman
Printed in China

5 4 3 2 1

Down East
BOOKS·MAGAZINE·ONLINE

If you wake up at dawn with a tail in your face,
   you can be pretty sure that you've run out of space.

      A family of beavers, in their lodge made of sticks,
         had a problem with room that nothing could fix.

So Barney and Bennie and Becky and Beau
   were told by Ma Beaver, "It's time that you go!"

"You've learned to cut trees, build a lodge and a dam.
   Pa Beaver and I taught you all that we can.

      It's time that you left and went out on your own
         to find a good mate and build a lodge home."

The youngsters split up, going different directions,
but young Beau just didn't quite make the connection.

First Barney went west,
where he found a fine stream.

Next Bennie went east,
to the pond of his dreams.

Then Becky went south to a burbling brook.
She knew it was perfect—it took just one look.

Beau tried to head north, but he couldn't go straight.
He zig-zagged around till the day got too late.

Alone in the dark, Beau lay down on the ground.
In a moment or two his sleep was quite sound.

"GET UP, YOU BIG LUMMOX! WHY ARE YOU HERE?"
A loud voice was yelling right into Beau's ear.

"I mean you no harm, sir.
I just want a home!"

"Well, this isn't the place.
I like being alone!
I'm a prickly guy—
do I make myself clear?
No neighbors for me!
NOW GET OUT OF HERE!"

Beau headed off, thinking,
"Now, there's a rude fellow!
It must be that porcupines
never are mellow!"

So Beau plodded on, seeking just the right spot—
a place that had water and trees (quite a lot)

Then he found a river, with plenty of trees—
but not too much water, just up to his knees.

"I'll build a dam here. Then the water will rise!
     Next, I'll build a lodge, one that's just the right size."

But Beau didn't know that the river he'd found was really a ditch **in the middle of town!**

He began to build slowly (it **was** his first try).
He mixed mud with branches and piled it up high.

He gathered some more sticks,
but they were too small.
Then he saw a **BIG** stick
just over a wall.

The stick that he'd found, so long and so round,
had a nasty big claw that stuck in the ground.

He pulled and he tugged till his head had an ache.
Beau didn't know that he'd just found a rake!

He pushed and he shoved, and got it in place.
It fit in his dam like a nose on a face.

Beau was so proud. "This isn't too tough
for a beaver like me! I'll go get **more** stuff!"

He scouted some more, and it wasn't too hard
to find even more useful things in the yard.

Beau spent several days hauling things that he found
back to that ditch in the middle of town.

The dam quickly grew, and was soon three feet tall,
thanks to all the good stuff he'd found over the wall.

His dam had a rake and a blue plastic truck,
a barbecue grill and a toy rubber duck.

He added more branches—it didn't take long—
but he needed a **tree** to make it real strong.

He found the right tree not too far away
and started in gnawing without a delay.

He gnawed on the left.

He gnawed on the right.

He gnawed in the middle with all of his might.

The tree finally fell, but not quite where it should.
It fell on a car—and smashed in the hood!

A man ran from the house, going fast as a shot.
"A beaver," he yelled, **"cannot live in this spot!"**

He ran to the phone to get help from the town.
"Hello, Beaver Control? Send someone right down!"

When the man stomped away, Beau went back to work piling more sticks, adding even more dirt.

He worked three more hours, adding more branches. The water was deep now, at least forty inches!

$\mathcal{B}$eau was proud of his dam in the river he'd found.
Too bad it was built **in the middle of town!**

The finishing touch was a branch short and thick.
Beau saw the right branch and grabbed at it quick!

The stick wouldn't budge. Then came a loud **snap!**
And Beau found himself caught inside a big trap!

The trap—with Beau in it—was put on a truck.
The truck drove for hours.... Was Beau out of luck?

The truck stopped. The trap opened. Beau hit the ground.
He opened one eye and looked carefully around.

A lovely young beaver stood looking at him.
"What is your name?" she asked. "Where have you been?"

"My name is Beau. I'm not sure where I've been.
But I know that I still need a home to live in."

"My name is Brenda. I need a home too.
    And I need a mate, and that mate could be YOU!
There's a big ruined lodge in a pond that's nearby—
    so let's fix it up, if you're willing to try."

"You're so kind and pretty. Sure, I'll be your mate.
    We'll fix up that lodge and make it **first rate!**"

So Brenda and Beau worked hard for a week
and rebuilt the lodge and fixed every leak.

Happy and safe in the pond they had found,
they were far, far away from the middle of town!

And Brenda and Beau are living there still,
in that nice, quiet pond just over the hill.

LEARN MORE ABOUT BEAVERS . . .

How big are beavers? What color are they?
Beavers weigh forty to ninety-five pounds and are three to four feet long (the flat tail is twelve to eighteen inches long). Beavers never stop growing and can live as long as twelve years. They are dark brown with a paler brown tummy. Their tails and feet are black.

Is the beaver's tail furry?
No. It has black, scaly skin with only a few stiff hairs. It looks like a paddle. A beaver uses its tail for steering when it swims and as a prop when it sits up. To warn other beavers of danger, a beaver will slap its tail on the surface of the water.

Beavers often groom each other.

The front feet are closed when swimming at the surface.

What about those big black feet?
The front feet have strong claws. The back feet have webs between the toes. When a beaver swims, it closes its front feet into fists and uses its back feet to push through the water.

Do beavers have many enemies?
The kits (babies) do, because they are small and could be lunch for otters, large fish, foxes, hawks, and owls. Adult beavers are in danger only from very large animals such as wolves, bears, wolverines, and bobcats. To keep safe, beavers like to work at night and in pairs. They are safest in the water and can stay under the surface for up to fifteen minutes.

A tail slap warns other beavers of danger.

Things beavers and humans have in common:
• They have five toes on all feet and use front feet to hold things.
• They live as a cooperative family; adults teach their young.
• They are superb engineers and can completely change their environment—taking down trees and building dams, which create ponds and regulate water flows to their benefit.

How do beavers build dams?

They use mud and stones or existing stumps to start. Then they add brush, more mud and stones, logs, and just about anything else they find. Dams have been found with deer antlers, railroad ties, cornstalks, and even a TV antenna used in their construction. Most dams are five feet high and may be any length. *The longest dam ever found is in Montana and is 2140 feet long!*

Do they *always* build dams?

No. If the water is already deep enough, they will just build a lodge. The reason they need deep water is so their lodge can be surrounded by water. Even the front and back doors to the lodge are under water. This keeps the beavers and their kits safe. Beavers are fast, strong swimmers, but they are slow and awkward on land.

Beavers often work in pairs. They use their teeth and front feet to pull branches into the water.

How do they build their lodges? What do they do in there?

Beavers build their lodges the same way they build dams, using mud, stones, and brush. The lodges stick up three to six feet above the water. They enter the lodge through underwater tunnels, but their "room" inside is above the water. There they can stay warm and dry. They bring in food and spend time grooming their beautiful fur by combing it with their front feet. A beaver uses oil from a special gland near its tail to make its fur shiny and *waterproof!*

Underwater tunnels provide a safe entrance to the lodge.

Those huge teeth! Are they really orange?

Yes, the big front teeth are orange. They also never stop growing! The outside surface of each tooth is very hard, while the inside surface is softer, so as a beaver gnaws on trees and its teeth wear down, they always stay sharp. A beaver can bring down a five-inch-diameter tree in three minutes!

Beavers use their front feet like hands.

What does it mean when Beau is "looking for a mate"?

Beau is looking for a female beaver to be his life partner and raise a family. Beavers stay with one mate for life. Their kits are born in April or May, usually two to four kits in a litter. The kits stay in their parents' lodge until they are two years old. Then they leave, as Beau did, to start their own home and family somewhere else.

What do beavers eat?

They eat the soft bark of the trees they cut down for building. Sometimes they will sit on their hind legs and munch around a branch the way a person eats corn on the cob. They also eat grasses, all kinds of water plants, ferns, berries, mushrooms, vegetables, and apples. They store food for the winter close to their underwater lodge, so even when their pond is covered with ice, they have their "groceries" handy!

Why do we say "busy as a beaver!"?

Because they are always repairing, constructing, cutting, and hauling. Beavers never quit!

Mother and kit munching on plants.